BIG TOES,

little toes

Open toes

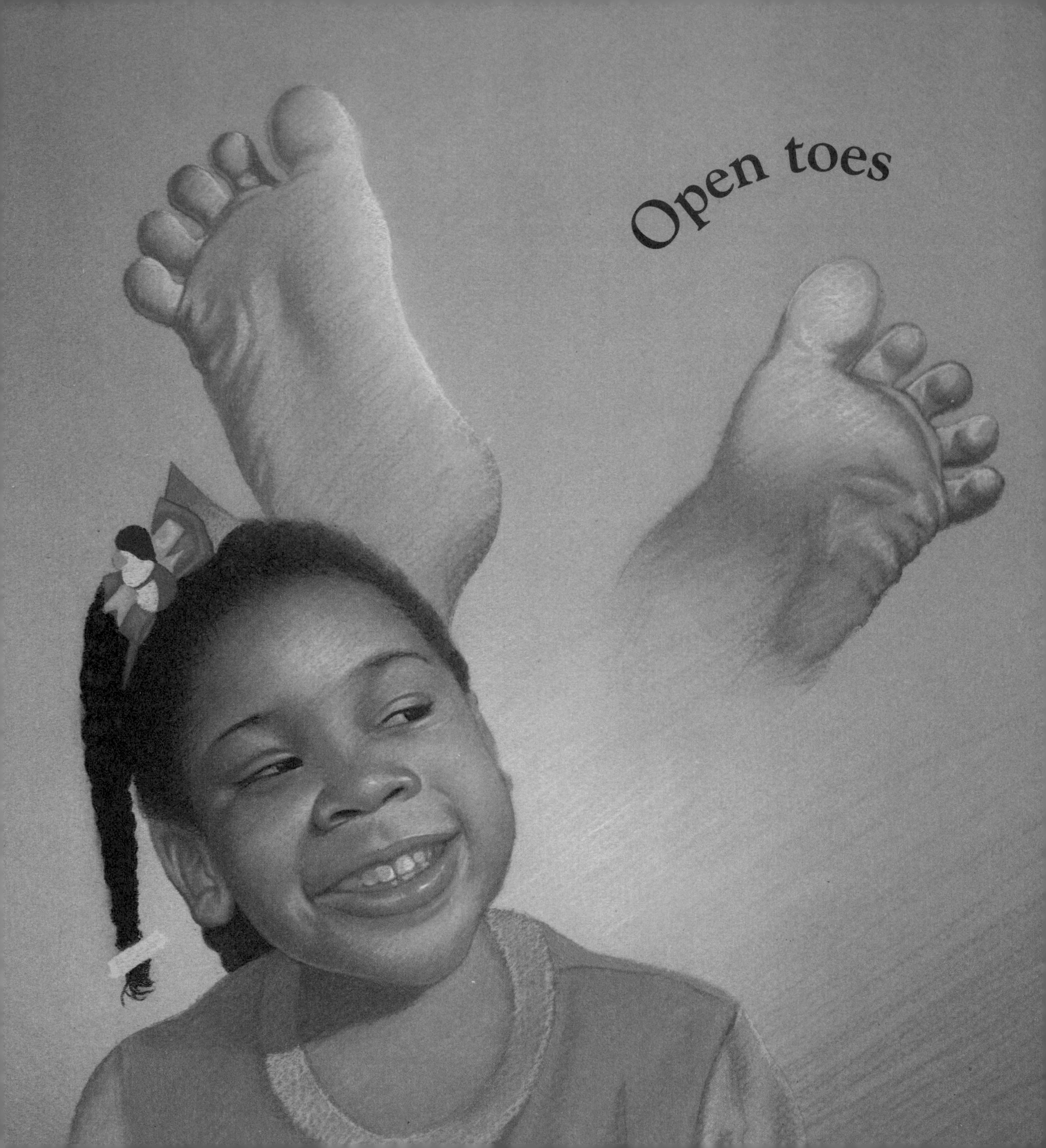

Busy Toes

Busy Toes

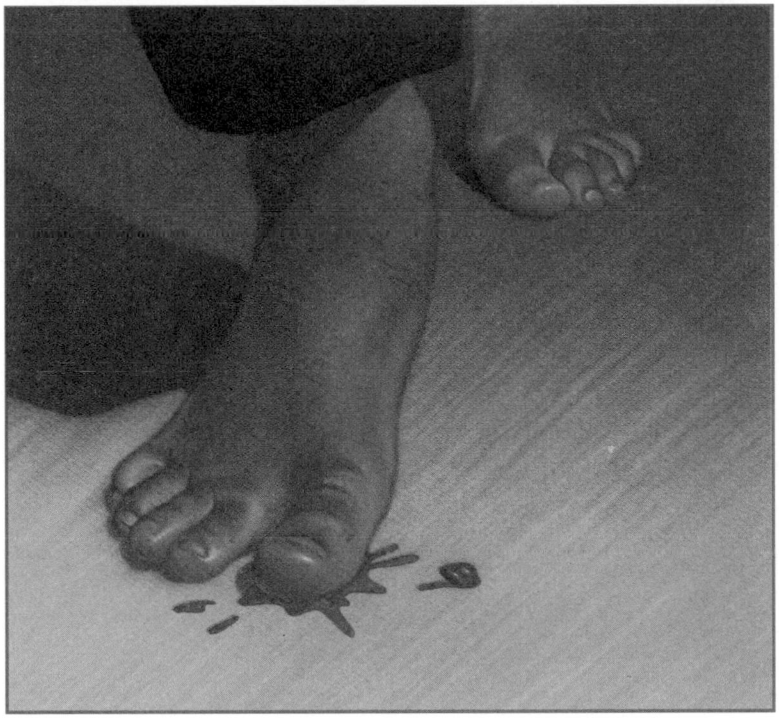

by C. W. Bowie

illustrated by

Fred Willingham

SCHOLASTIC INC.

New York Toronto London Auckland Sydney
Mexico City New Delhi Hong Kong

For my husband, who always knew I'd be published one day
—W.O.

Although all eleven of my grandchildren have very busy toes, I dedicate this book especially to Haley and Jackson Eargle and Michael McGonigle
—M. B-K.

To my father, Count Gibson, who taught me to write with my toes
—C.G.W.

To my girls, Desirée and Nikkia
—F.W.

ISBN 0-439-17874-6

12 11 10 9 8 7 6 5 4 1 2 3 4 5/0

Printed in the U.S.A. 09

First Scholastic printing, February 2000

Text was set in 30-point Goudy Bold.
Book design by *The Kids at Our House*

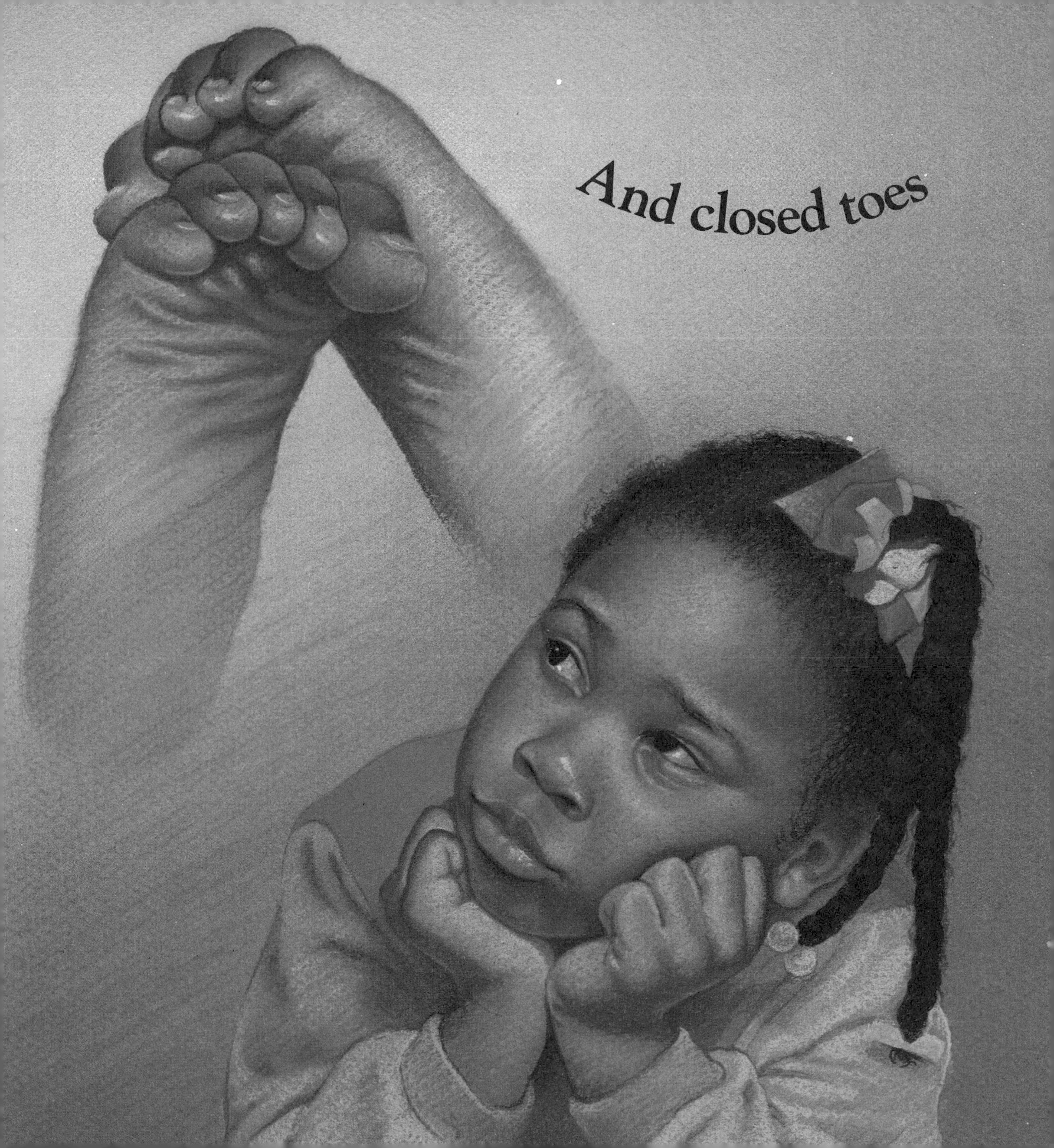

And closed toes

Waving toes

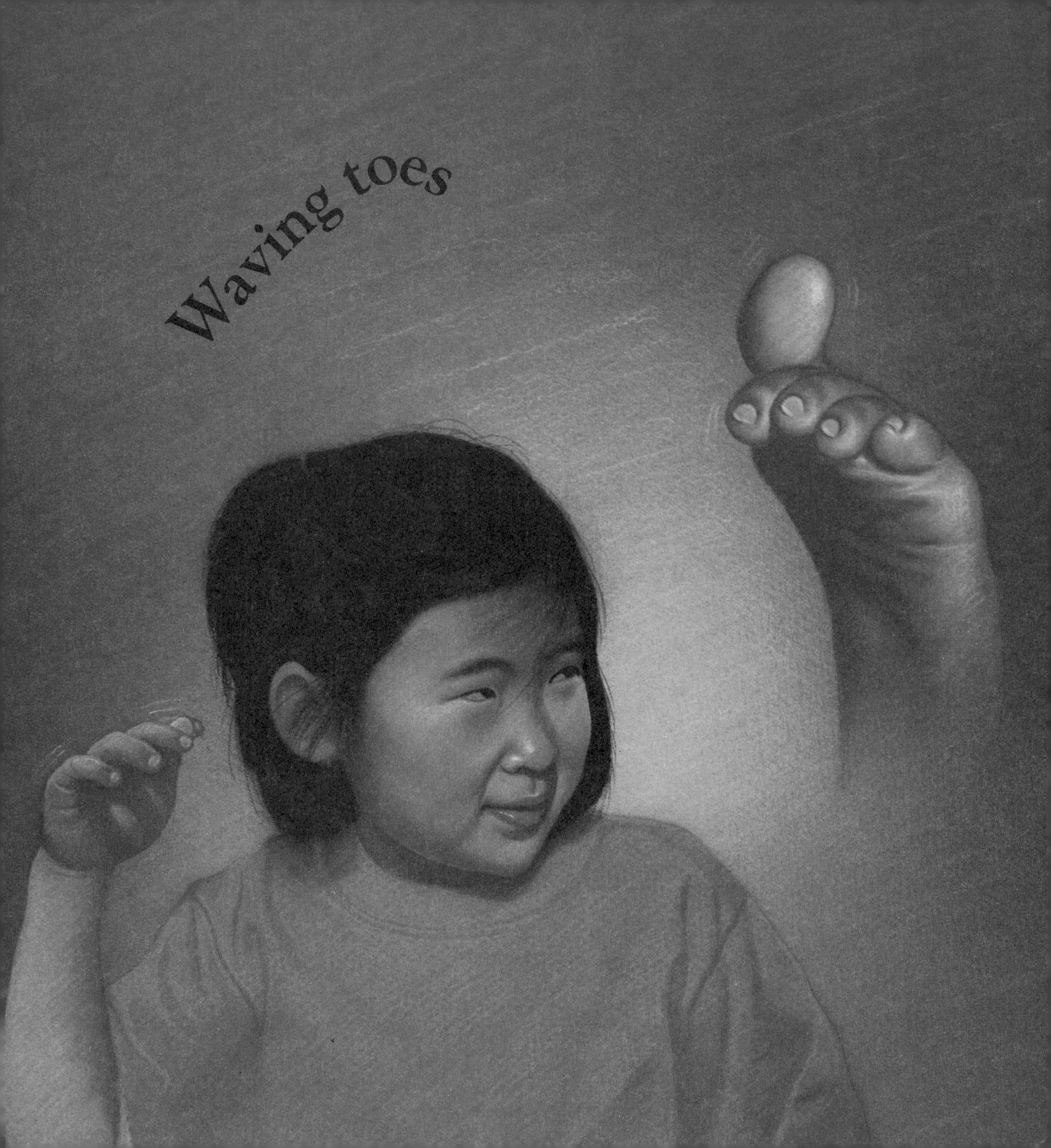

Tickling toes

Doggy tummy rubbing toes

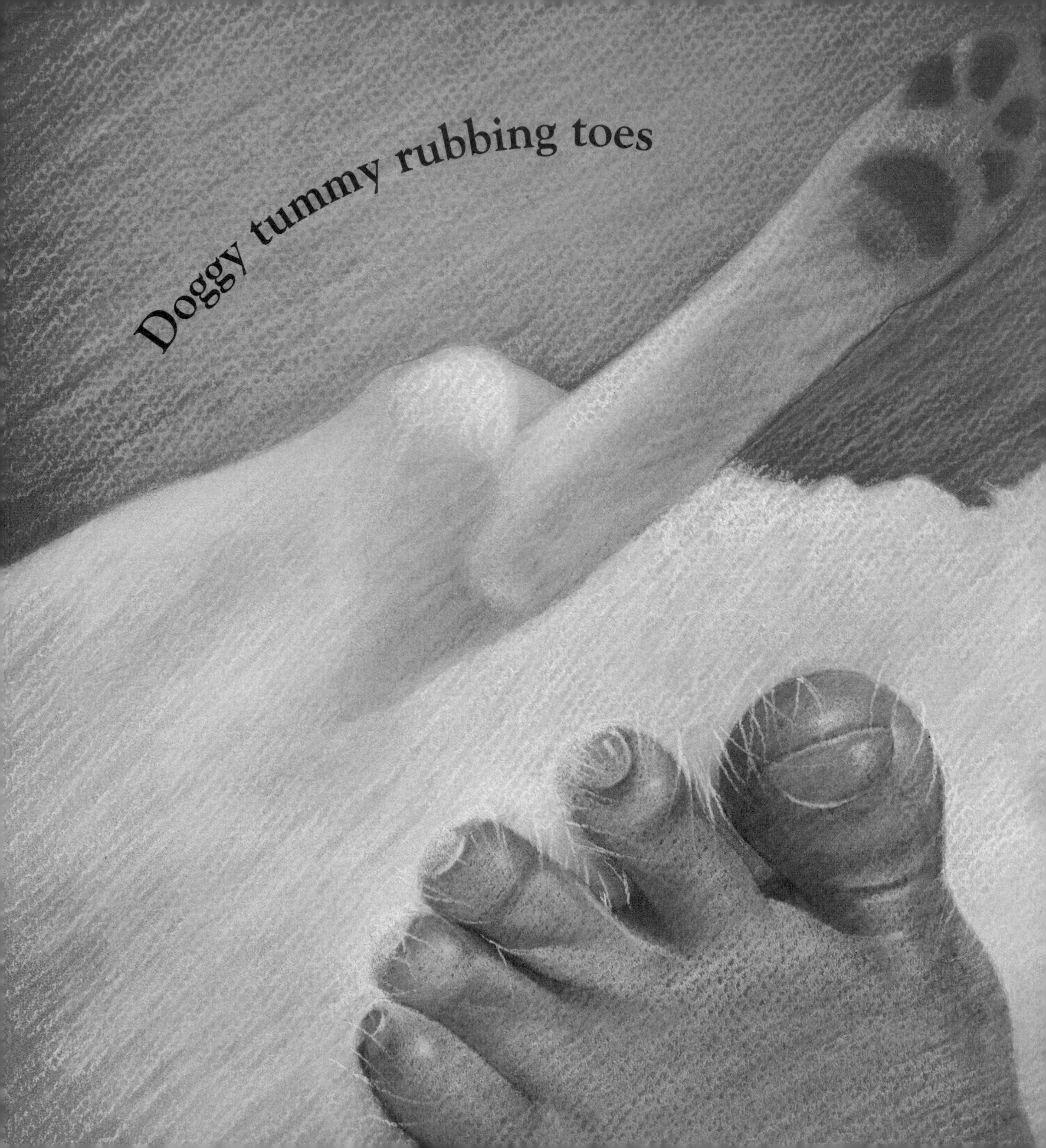

Drawing toes

Digging toes

Hidden toes

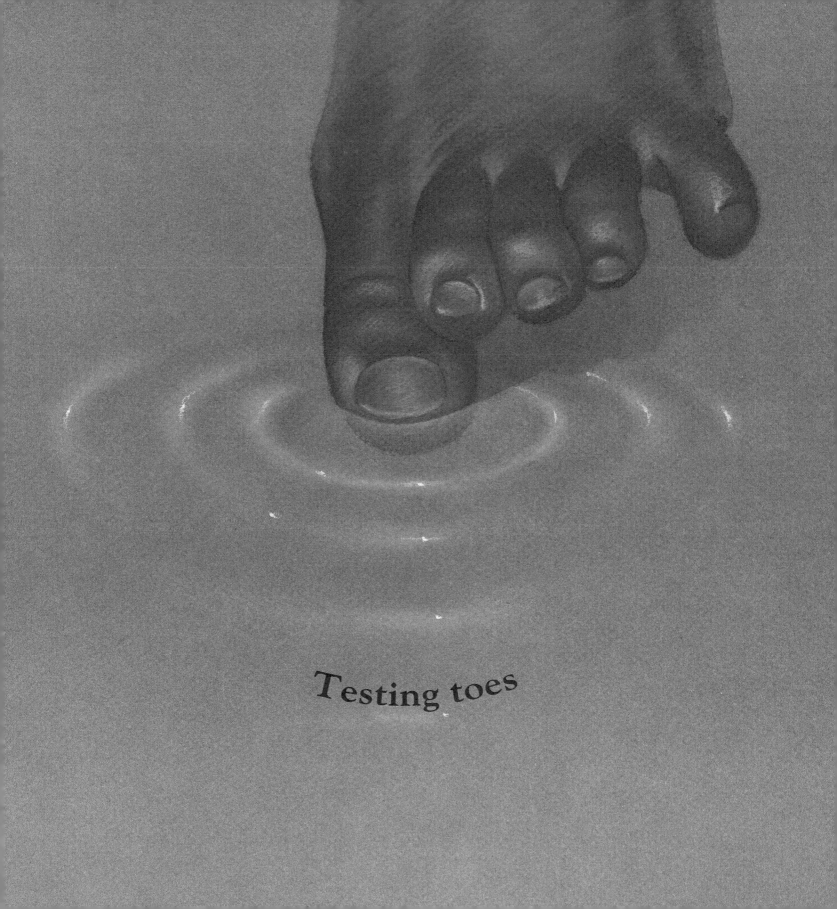

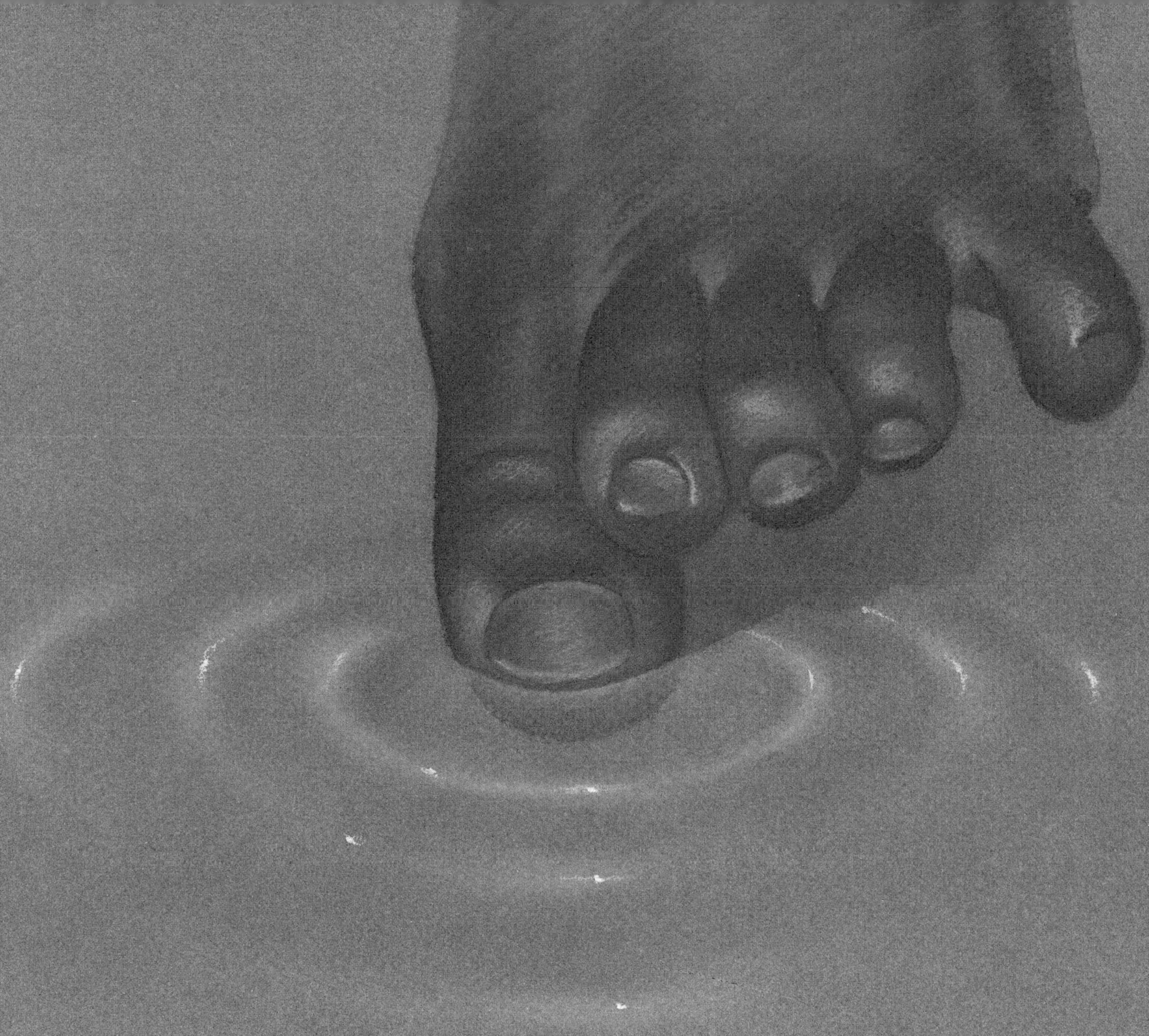

Testing toes

Splashing toes

Squishing toes

And don't forget
the fishing toes

Tippy toes and
dancing toes

Tasting toes

Counting toes

Pick-up toes

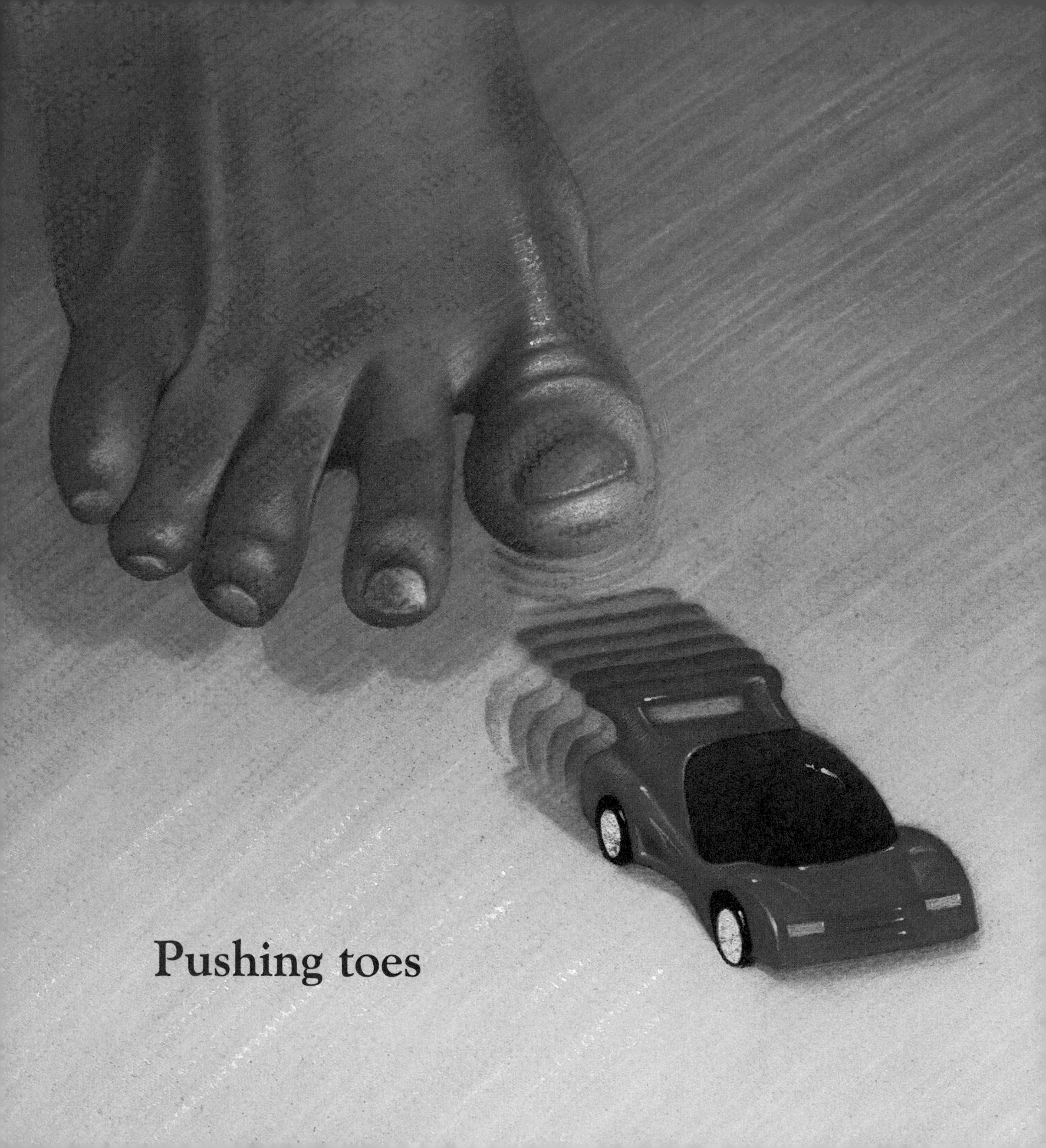

Pushing toes

Wearing *teeny*
clothes on toes

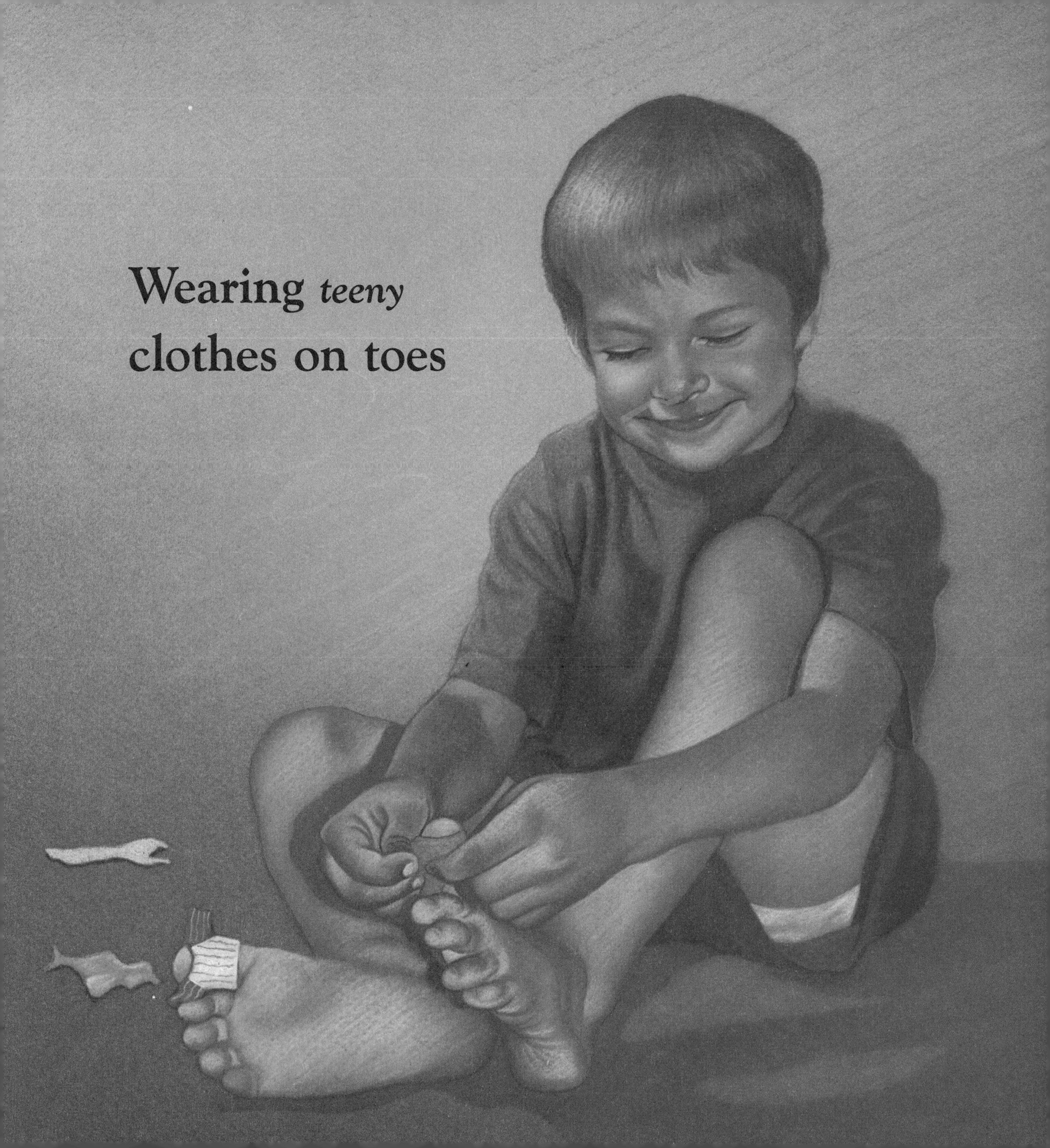

Soapy toes

Shadow toes

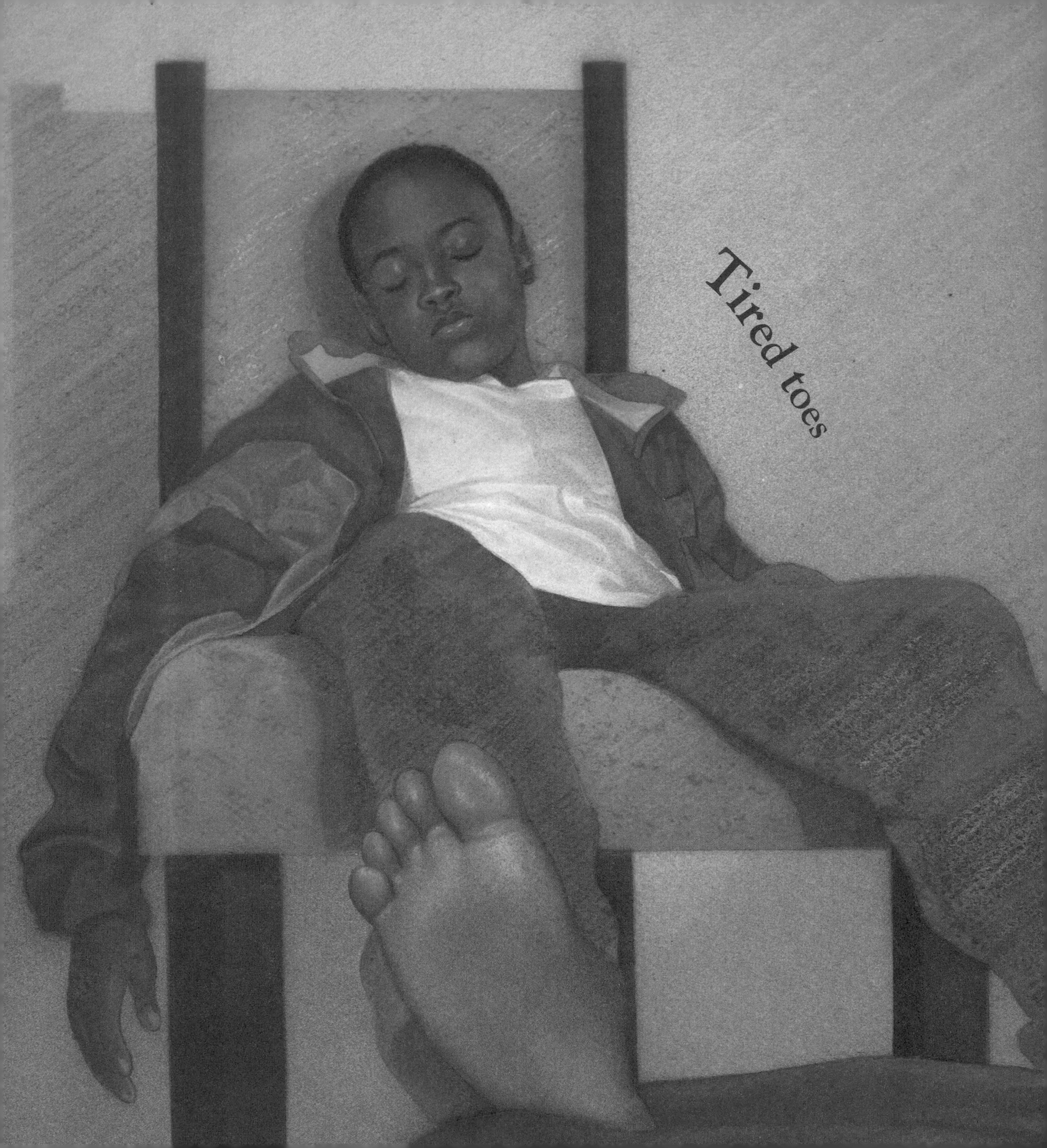

Tired toes

And tent toes

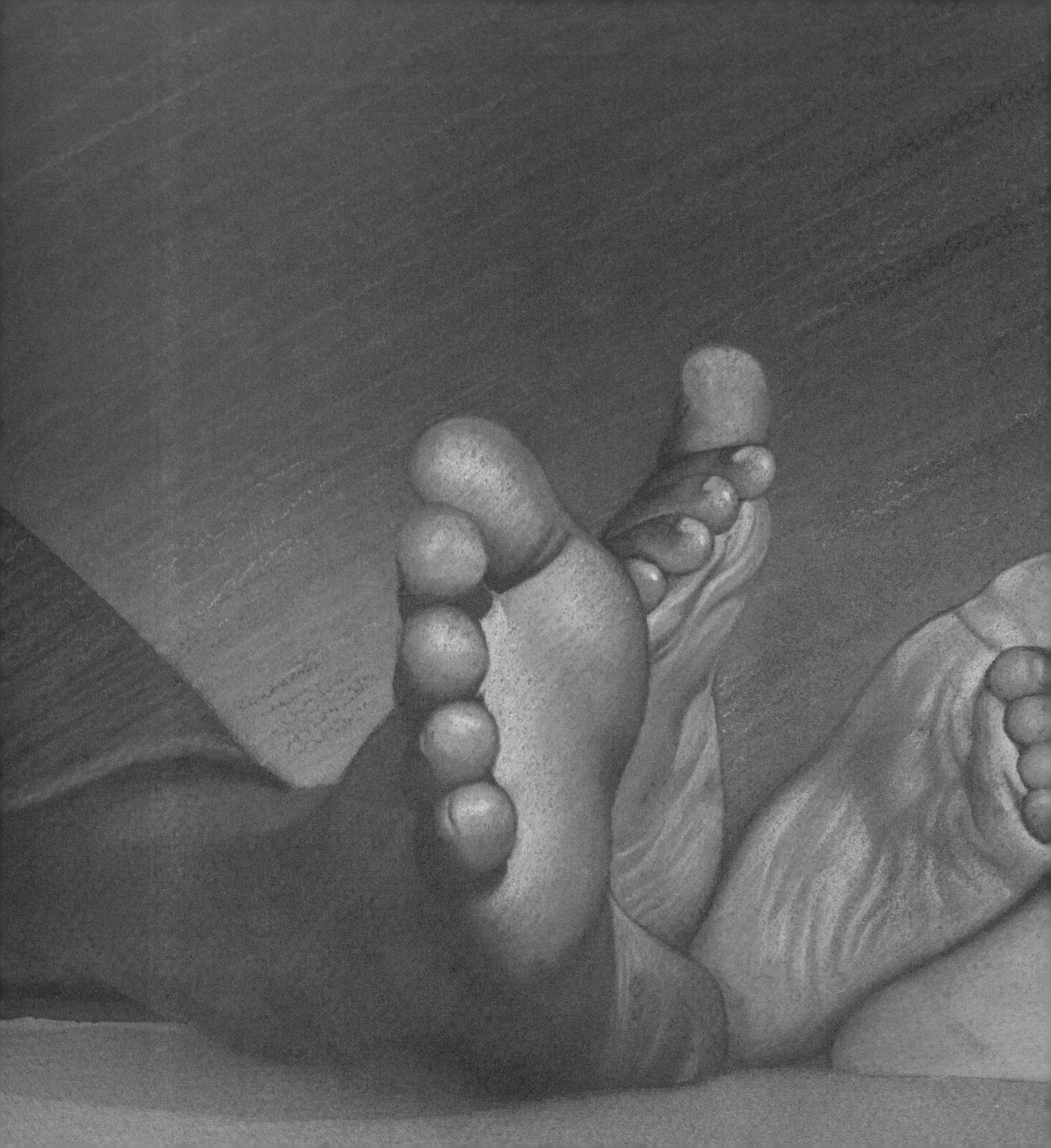

Kissing, cuddling, loving toes . . . and

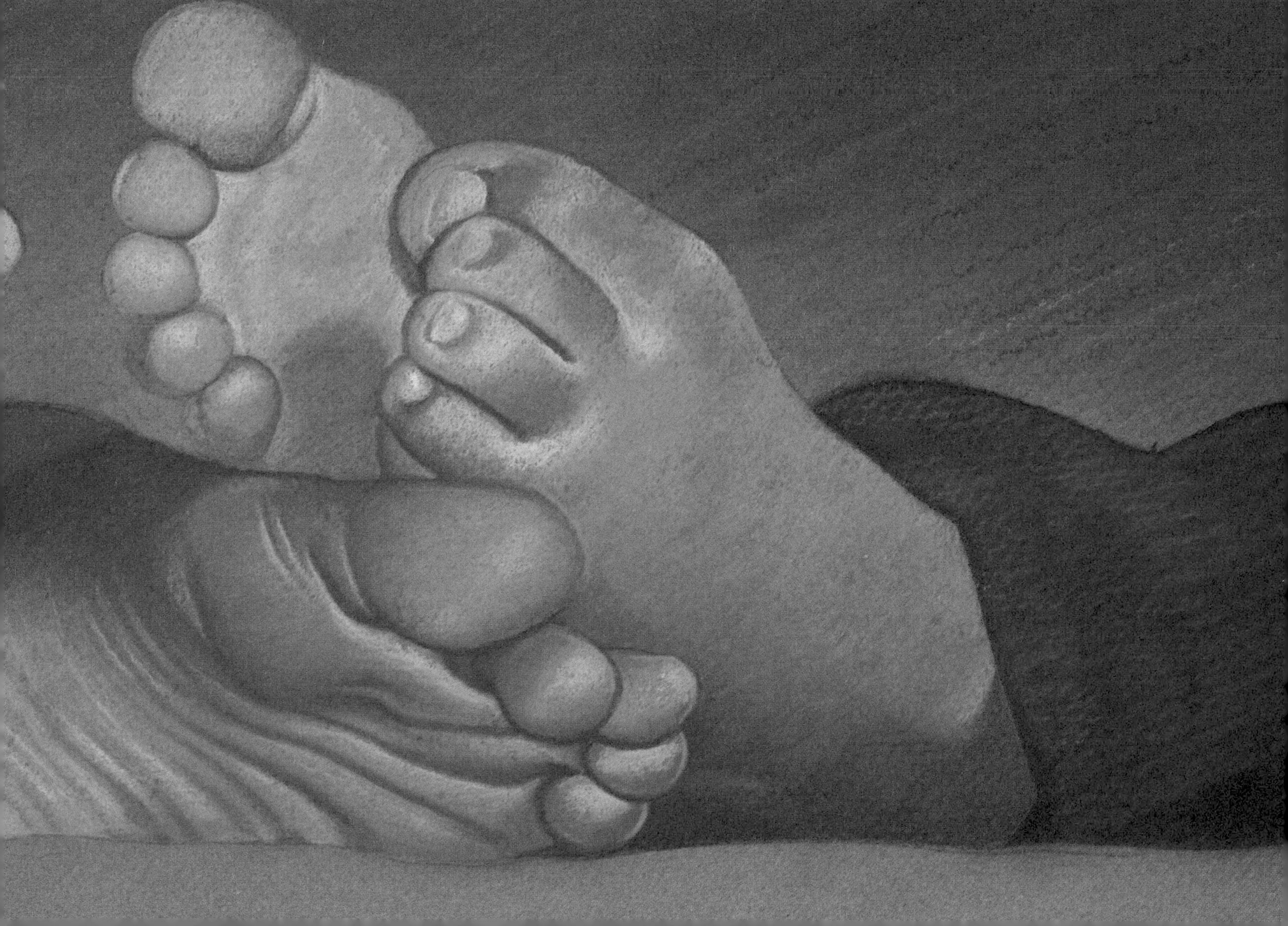

Goodnight, toes!